What's Up, Maloo?

Geneviève Godbout

tundra

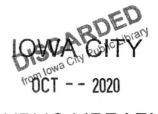

One hop. Two hops. Three hops.
No other kangaroo can hop like Maloo!

Hop!

Hop!

Hop!

Hop?

One step. Two steps. Three steps.
What's up, Maloo?

Four steps. Five steps. Six steps.
What's wrong, Maloo?

Seven steps. Eight steps. Nine steps.
Let us help you, Maloo.

Hold on tight, Maloo!

Plop.

Ten steps . . . one hundred steps . . .
one thousand steps . . .

Hop?

You can do it, Maloo!

Hop!

Hop!

Hop!

Hop-hop-hurray!
Let's all hop like Maloo!

Hop!

To Seï and her fog that I didn't know how to see

Text and illustrations copyright © 2018 by Geneviève Godbout
Originally published in French by Les Éditions de la Pastèque in 2018.

Published in English by Tundra Books in 2020.

Tundra Books, an imprint of Penguin Random House Canada Young Readers,
a Penguin Random House Company

Library and Archives Canada Cataloguing in Publication
Title: What's up, Maloo? / Geneviève Godbout.
Other titles: Malou. English | What is up, Maloo?
Names: Godbout, Geneviève, author, illustrator.
Description: Translation of: Malou.
Identifiers: Canadiana (print) 20190094192 | Canadiana (ebook) 20190094206 |
ISBN 9780735266643 (hardcover) | ISBN 9780735266650 (EPUB)
Classification: LCC PS8613.O283 M3413 2020 | DDC jC843/.6—dc23

Published simultaneously in the United States of America by Tundra Books
of Northern New York, an imprint of Penguin Random House Canada Young
Readers, a Penguin Random House Company

Library of Congress Control Number: 2019938673

The artwork in this book was rendered in pastels and colored pencils.
The text was set in a typeface based on hand-lettering by Geneviève Godbout.

Printed and bound in China

www.penguinrandomhouse.ca

1   2   3   4   5   24   23   22   21   20

Penguin
Random House
TUNDRA BOOKS